The Deer Hunting Book

Short stories for young hunters

Michael Waguespack

First edition 2013
Country Kid Publishing
www.countrykidpublishing.blogspot.com

ISBN-10 0975462466
ISBN-13 978-0-9754624-6-1

Printed in the USA

The Stories

10 Commandments of Weapon Safety

— Treat every weapon as though it is loaded.
— Always keep the weapon pointed in a safe direction. Never at people.
— Be sure of your target before you pull the trigger or release.
— Never point a weapon at anything you don't plan to shoot.
— Never shoot at a flat, hard surface or water.
— Never climb or jump with a loaded weapon.
— Unload a weapon when it is not being used.
— Keep weapons clear and clean.
— Store weapons and ammunition separately.
— Avoid alcohol and drugs before and during shooting.

Dear Reader,

I grew up both an enthusiastic reader and deer hunter. For me, the excitement of finding a good story was on par with spotting a buck in the woods. Yet, hunting books for kids were—and still are—hard to find.

I wrote this collection of stories thinking about my young reading and hunting self. Some stories are inspired by actual hunts from my youth. Others are more like tall tales inspired by adventures I imagined during long days in a treestand.

My hope is that you'll find these stories familiar and entertaining. I hope your pulse quickens a few times. Maybe you'll smile a little, too. Perhaps you'll be inspired to grab a piece of paper and write a story of your own. And in the end, we'll have continued these wonderful traditions —storytelling and hunting—together.

Good luck on the hunt,
Michael Waguespack

Settle Down

And there he is. The giant buck I've been waiting for. My breath sucks in. My heart pumps faster. My face grows hot.

I'd been sweeping my gaze back and forth from brush to trees to field, and I hadn't seen a sign under my treestand all evening. It is as if he's appeared out of nowhere. Standing there, forty-five yards away, looking into the field. Broadside.

I hadn't heard anything except the chirps and tweets of autumn birds playing in the branches and the fallen leaves. I'd been thinking about cutting out early. As the sun dropped to just over the trees, the chill in the light breeze had stabbed through my thermals and refrigerated my bones. I'd kept telling myself, "I can wait one more minute." I knew that just before dark was when they moved the most.

And what a reward for sticking it out! A giant 10 pointer just a shot away.

I grip my rifle tightly, raising the butt to my shoulder. Slow and steady.

Well, slow and earthquake-shaky is more like it. I tell myself to settle down, but the thrill is beyond holding back. There's a headline for you: "Kid Hunter Gets so Excited He Drops Gun Out of Treestand".

I squint an eye into my scope. I try to place the crosshairs, but at first all I get are blurs of fur sweeping in and out of my telescoped view as if I'm in a boat at sea instead of the seat of my treestand.

I close my eyes. *Settle down, dang it. Act like you've seen this movie before.* That's the advice Dad always gives me when he thinks I am over-excited about something. But this isn't a movie, and I've never been this excited.

I take a long breath and count to eight. Then, I open my eyes and breathe out slowly.

There, that is better. Not perfect, but now the fur stays in the scope. *Don't look at the antlers*, I coach myself. I know that will kick me into earthquake-shake mode again.

The buck tips his nose a bit, and a cloud of breath puffs into the cold air. It is his first movement since he magically appeared. Up to this point I could have mistaken him for a stuffed statue. He puffs another foggy breath. Has he caught a scent? My scent?

I trace an imaginary line up his leg, and I set the crosshairs over his heart.

I fight to keep my breathing smooth and the crosshairs stable.

I curl my finger into the trigger.

Another easy breath.

Squeeze the trigger.

Buh-Bang!

The shot explodes in my ears as the rifle kicks into my shoulder, though I hardly notice those things at all.

I watch the buck flinch and shift before whirling and charging into the brush. He makes it down into the small hollow and halfway up the other side before he stumbles and falls lifeless to the ground.

I let out the breath I hadn't realized I'd been holding. I let a small grin creep across my face.

My first downed buck.

I grab my cell phone out of my pocket and call Dad with shaky hands.

"Did you get one?" He says, skipping right past hello. He is in his treestand about 100 yards over, so my shot would have been hard to miss.

"Yeah, I have one down over here." I try to sound calm so that I won't hear that favorite line of his again, *Settle down. Act like you've seen this movie before.*

"That's awesome, Bud. What is it?" he asks.

I smile into the phone. "A deer."

"Funny. Seriously, buck or doe."

"Buck," I say.

"Really. That's awesome. How big?" I hear his excitement growing.

I have to tell him. "He's a 10 pointer, Dad. A total monster."

"Ten points. Wa-hoo!" I pull the phone from my ear and can hear his holler straight across the woods from his treestand.

"Geez, Dad. Settle down. Act like you've seen this movie before."

I chuckle into the phone and then wonder how long I have to wait for my jelly-legs to stabilize before I can climb down and go see my buck.

Dear Dad

November 2nd

Dear Dad,

I hope you are safe over there. I sure miss you. Mom is telling me to tell you "hi" and "to send you kisses and hugs". I just told her that she's gross and to send her own kisses, so we're both laughing right now.

Anyway, like you asked me to do, I'm gonna fill you in on everything about deer season this year. I know you said you can't check your email until your weekend patrol is over; so I guess youth weekend is over as you're reading. Man, I hope there's exciting emails from me already waiting after this one.

Like I told you, I've been target shooting every weekend since you were deployed in October. I'm not wanting to brag too much, but tell your sniper buddies to let me know if they need any advice. Haha.

Seriously, yesterday, I shot the bull's-eye completely out. And only one bullet hit just outside the bull's-eye line. I'm so excited about it, but wish you were here to slap me on the back and tell me, "Good job, Buddy!" like you always do.

And—I can't believe I didn't start with this —guess who I caught on the trail cam last week? Ole Big Typ. He's back and he's even bigger than last year. I bet he's got another inch on his tines compared to that shed we found. He was over there entering the clearing by the creek at about 2 am. Hopefully, he'll come by me chasing some does in the daytime while I'm in my stand tomorrow. Wouldn't that be awesome?

By the way, you'd be proud of Mom for not complaining about having to be the adult with me for youth season. She did tell me I couldn't make her wear deer pee. I guess she thought we put it on like cologne or something. I have to admit it is kind of cool being the expert about that kind of stuff. In a way, it's like she's the kid, and I'm the parent. I told her if she spooks my deer away that she'll be grounded for a month. Haha.

I guess I better finish getting my gear ready and go act like I'm actually going to be able to sleep tonight. I totally wish you could be the one with me in the buddy stand again this year, but I'll try to make you proud anyway.

Love you Dad,

Jackson

P.S. I'll be safe. You be safe, too.

November 3rd

Dear Dad,

Well, we saw him. Ole Big Typ came out at about 7:45. You know, that time in the morning that I tell you my toes are officially frozen. Haha. And yet what happened wasn't funny at all.

He came to the edge of the clearing about 60 yards from the treestand. I raised my gun, but he'd stopped behind a sapling that blocked my shot. He watched the field for what seemed like forever. He didn't look real; he stood still for so long. And, through the scope I forgot what you told me about ignoring the antlers and started counting those tines. They were so perfect, Dad. It made me more excited and nervous than I've ever been before; so my arms started shaking real bad even though I was using the gunrest. I did like you said and relaxed the gun down and took long deep breaths in and long breaths out which really did help make my shakes go away.

I looked over at Mom, and she was smiling with fingers in her ears, ready for my shot.

Which was about the time Ole Big Typ stepped out. Just two or three steps forward and he stopped again, broadside with an open shot for me. So, I exhaled as I eased the gun back up to my shoulder, being careful not to stare at the antlers. I swore I wouldn't go buck fever again.

And, that's when I saw my problem. I had totally fogged up the scope. I guess I'd breathed out my deep breaths right onto the glass as I had relaxed. The lens was so fogged up it looked like I was aiming into a thick puffy cloud.

I should have dropped my eyes down to the open sight and took my shot. But instead I decided a quick wipe of the lens would fix the problem. Of course, as I was doing that I accidentally clanged my grunt call against the rifle. Just a tiny little click-clack noise was all it took. Ole Big Typ didn't even look over or up at me. He just whirled around and charged off. Gone.

No matter what Mom tells you, those weren't tears she saw. Just a speck of dust or something that had blown into my eye.

We stayed in the treestand for several more hours this morning and this afternoon, but didn't even see a doe. Just a stray cat. (Mom enjoyed that. She whispered, "Oh, look a kitty.")

I'm just so mad at myself. The "buck of a lifetime" as you say, and I blew it.

That's all I have. We'll go back out tomorrow, but I don't expect to see him again. Ever.

Love you Dad,

Jackson

P.S. I'll be safe. You be safe, too.

November 4th

Dear Dad,

You aren't going to believe this. We saw him again! Ole Big Typ. But this time it was on our way into the stand before daylight. We did a slow, quiet pace like we always do, and I heard something up ahead so we just stopped and listened. I thought it might be a squirrel down in the leaves early. I don't know, maybe a opossum. But then I heard a low grunt. Well, that got my heart pumping. So, I eased us over to lean our backs against a big tree that was right near us. Mom was ninja-quiet the whole time. I was so impressed.

I didn't grunt back since we were on the ground, and it wasn't that close to shooting time yet. There was just a little blue glow on the eastern horizon. Maybe five minutes went by and I heard another grunt, this time off to the side out in the hayfield above the clearing. Maybe 100 yards away, I guess.

Even if it was light enough to see that far I couldn't have because you know how there's that hilly spot blocking the tree line across the field. Maybe ten minutes later, it was lighter, and I saw a doe come fast-walking up over the hill and angle across the ridge of the field.

I was excited to see a deer but I didn't have a shot, and I wasn't ready to shoot a doe anyway with the buck grunts I'd just heard. Which was smart, because moments later those tall familiar tines came following that doe along as Ole Big Typ emerged over that bump in the field. I hadn't spooked him that bad yesterday after all.

I never had a shot or anything through the brambly underbrush, I just watched him come up and over into full view and walk out of the field after that doe. To tell you the truth, I was pretty much relieved that I'd seen him again and didn't mess anything up this time. We did hurry-sneak to the stand after that. I tried to grunt him back in. But I didn't hear anything from him the rest of the morning. We did have a spike come out, but, you know, we'd decided not to shoot the young ones so I let him pass.

Mom thought it was cool to see him though, which was fun. I'm kind of hoping I get another chance at Ole Big Typ again this afternoon. Maybe that's hoping for too much.

Write you again tonight.

Love you Dad,

Jackson

P.S. I'll be safe. You be safe, too.

November 4th, Afternoon

Dear Dad,

Holy cow (or holy deer, I guess), have I got a story for you.

First of all, I think Mom is totally hooked on hunting now. Next year, we're going to need a three-seater stand. Haha. She's also telling me to send you more hugs and kisses, right now. Did you know it is kind of hard to type and make the gagging gesture at the same time?

Anyway, after lunch I got Mom to take me out right away so instead of sitting from 3:30pm like yesterday, we were out at just after 2:00pm. What a great idea. Except that there wasn't a single deer to be seen. One hour. two hours. Three hours. Not even the stray cat came back by.

So, by the time the sun started to hit the trees to the west, I was pretty discouraged. And my butt and legs were half asleep. You'd be proud of Mom. She didn't say a word about leaving early. It was me who was thinking of giving up.

But then, way across on the other side of the hayfield, beyond the clearing, a pair of does walked out. It would have been a pretty long shot, but I went ahead and pulled my rifle to my shoulder and put them in my scope. They were grazing and slowly making their way in our direction, so I just waited patiently to get a better shot and settle myself a little as my heart was beating pretty good.

Then, out from where the does had come, a buck stepped out. Seeing antlers got some shaking going along with my pounding chest. I knew immediately it was not Ole Big Typ. This one was a solid 8 pointer that I'd be proud to tag, though.

I looked over at Mom to see if she'd seen the buck. She had. I could tell by her "Oh, wowser" wide-open eyes. And she was plugging her ears again. I grinned and turned back to my scope.

He was coming in really slow and facing me. It was a distant shot—over 100 yards. And even though I was doing my deep breaths (not into the scope this time), I wasn't confident in pulling the trigger yet. I had to let him come in closer and hoped he'd turn broadside for a better target. The only trouble was that the sun was almost totally down behind the trees. My light wasn't going to last.

As the light continued to dim, the does got to only 50 yards out before they left the main field and entered the clearing in front of us. The buck had eased in to about 75 yards, and it was time to make a decision.

I squinted my shooting eye down the scope and let out a deep breath as I steadied my shakes and set the crosshairs up onto his chest. I began to curl my trigger finger and...

Gonk! Mom gave me an elbow, almost making me blow the shot.

I looked at her and mouthed, "What was that!"

But her "Oh wowser!" eyes were super double-wide now as she was pointing down to the ground below us.

I dropped my gaze and found myself with a satellite view of the biggest set of antlers I've ever seen. Ole Big Typ had snuck in right under the treestand! I was surprised my thumping heart didn't scare him away; it seemed so loud. Sweat began to wet my forehead despite it still being super chilly out there.

Dad, we've never talked about where or how to shoot a deer when you're suspended directly above it, so I had to just sit there and wait. Wait! With him right there. I mean, I could have slipped out of my safety harness and jumped down onto his back.

But it didn't take long. He was watching those does and the other buck and started walking toward them, making tending grunts as he went. At about 20 yards out, I put him in my scope, but all I had was a shot at his rear end. So, I gave a whispery puff into my grunt call.

He stopped, and his head spun to the right. Still, no shot. The light had faded more so that the gray of the dead leaves began to blend with his fur, especially with the lighter field silhouetted behind him. I gave another quiet half puff of a grunt. He tipped his snout for a quick sniff then slowly turned broadside to look my way.

I didn't really think. I aimed. I was steady. I squeezed the trigger.

"Ka-pow!" The rifle recoiled into my shoulder, and I lost sight of him through the scope. I pulled the rifle down and looked out there without the scope. The blur of white tails streaked out of the back of the clearing as the does and 8 pointer retreated.

But right there in front of me, at the edge of the woods, was Ole Big Typ lying motionless.

Dad, I really got him! He dropped right there. The buck of a lifetime is my first buck!

Mom was all hyper excited and not only helped me field dress him, but let me drive the truck down to get him. Which was kind of silly because the two of us didn't even come close to lifting him. We had to call the Wilsons to come over. They, of course, couldn't believe their eyes and said they'd never seen such a big and perfect rack. They said they didn't even know we had deer like that around here.

Anyway, I'm gonna go now. I wish you could have been here, but it sure has been fun getting to tell you the story.

Next year, I bet you'll be home, and Mom and I can help you get Ole Big Typ's little brother. Haha.

Love you Dad,

Jackson

P.S. I was safe. You be safe, too.

Hunting Bananas

Every year on opening day of deer season, Dad gets me up at 4am. "Wake up, Sweet Girl," he says, shaking my leg.

I stumble into the kitchen while rubbing my eyes, and he cuts me a piece of his homemade ooey gooey buttercake. He puts the plate down in front of me and tells me not to tell Mom about getting dessert for breakfast, even though she's already sitting right there drinking her coffee.

The sugar gets me going and soon I've got my "Chef Chloe" hat on, and dad has his "Welcome to my Show" one on.

Every year we make a pot of banana-cinnamon oatmeal while Dad acts like a TV chef. He talks to an invisible camera while showing me how to do super easy things like peel a banana, and he makes up a new story every year about where the bananas came from.

Last year he said, "Look here as Lady Chloe prepares the secret ingredient." He looked both ways over his shoulders, then whispered, "Buh-na-nuh" in a sing-song voice. Then he went on a five minute rant about rafting down a river in Costa Rica and stealing that particular perfect bunch of bananas from the clutches of a ferocious baby monkey.

It's hilarious and wonderful and the absolute best opening morning tradition ever.

But not this year. This year my aunt is having her baby early so my cousins, Russ and Liz, are here. We usually only see each other at family get together stuff, so it is kind of weird having them stay. Russ is a month younger than me but treats me like a younger sister. Liz is only five with a whole heap of adorable and annoying piled on in equal parts.

We're all at the table and Dad just put down our plates of ooey gooey buttercake.

"Don't tell your, Mom," he says, like always.

Russ pipes up, "I think she already knows, she's sitting right there. No offense."

And Liz, scrunches her nose. "Ew. I don't like this," even though she hasn't even tried it.

I sit there frowning, echoing Liz's remark in my thoughts. *I don't like this either.*

Then Dad plops chef hats on us all and says to the invisible camera, "Oh, what a special treat we have for you today. Two extra chefs. Welcome to the show Chef Liz and Chef Russ."

They just sit and look at Dad like he is crazy. I lean over and whisper, "He means you get to help cook."

Russ says, "Cook? I can't cook. Cooking is for girls." Then he shoots a look at Dad. "No offense."

I say, "Nuh-uh. My mom is a girl, and she's the worst cook ever." I smile at Mom. "No offense."

She smiles back. "None taken." She hates cooking and isn't afraid to tell us about it on a regular basis. She continues, "I am a horrible cook, Russ. I could mess up a glass of milk."

Liz giggles. "You don't cook a glass of milk. You pour it."

"Oh, so that's my problem," Mom says, and smiles into her coffee cup.

Liz decides to help us cook and actually does a pretty good job listening to directions.

Russ just sits at the table and watches. I think he can't believe that Dad is really the cook in our house. Or that his sister and I are having so much fun helping.

Dad is going on about the special ingredient. "I risked my life to secure these buh-na-nuhs. I dog-sledded up to the peak of Everest and snowshoed down the other side into the Cave of Tropical Fruit. Then I snatched them from the clutches of a sleeping yeti. Cooking tip number 23, Liz. Never wake a yeti."

I smile, feeling the tradition finally getting back to normal.

"Bananas don't grow on Mount Everest," Russ interrupts.

Urgh. I want to yell at him to stop ruining my morning.

Dad just smiles. "Yes, I know. That's why the yetis store them in the Cave of Tropical Fruit after they steal them from Bigfoot down in the jungle. Duh."

Russ shakes his head. "There's no such thing as Bigfoot."

I'm seriously thinking about choking Russ when Liz grabs my arm and whispers, "My brother has big feet just like my mom."

And it is so adorable I'm able to keep myself from strangling her big-foot brother.

After we finish eating, Mom says, "We better go get our hunting clothes on. Russ, I put your gear in the downstairs bathroom. Chloe, you can get ready with me in my bedroom."

Russ looks annoyed. "She's going? Only boys are supposed to hunt. No offense."

I make a fist and am thinking about using it. *I'll show him offense!*

Mom chuckles. "Girls hunt, too. In our house, only the girls."

Russ looks positively offended as he glances over at Dad cleaning dishes. "Uncle Ron, you're not taking me hunting?"

Dad shrugs. "Only if we're hunting buh-na-nuhs."

Mom and I laugh.

Liz's face is scrunched. "No banana hunting, Uncle Ron. You said we're making chocolate chip cookies."

Russ sighs and then shuffles off to get dressed.

While Mom and I are getting dressed, I complain a bunch, but Mom tells me to chill out and that Russ is just trying to act like a know-it-all because he's actually totally stupid about hunting. Well, she said it in a nicer, aunt sort of way, but the point was that he'd never been deer hunting before let alone gotten one. He was supposed to go hunting with somebody else but with his mom in the hospital we got stuck with him.

I tell her he'll probably mess up our hunt like Dad did when he went with us those times. She says that would be okay because we were really just trying to help Russ not worry about his mom at the hospital. That does make me want to cut him a tiny break. If it was Mom in the hospital, I would probably be an accidental jerk, too. But if he messes up our hunt, I know I'll be an on purpose jerk, for sure.

Two hours later, the sun is up, and I'm loving being back in the outdoors. We haven't seen any deer yet, but it's just so refreshing sitting out there in the deer blind. It would be better if Russ wasn't there, but I have to say he is not annoying me right now.

I had been expecting a miniature version of Dad who couldn't sit still. However, Russ is sitting quietly with very little movements. Dad played games on his phone. Russ watches for prey like a predator. Dad would have been chilly an hour ago and asked for the keys to the truck. But even though it is pretty cold today, Russ hasn't complained once.

I pull out the chocolate bar I've been saving. I unwrap a corner quietly and break off a square. I tap Russ on the shoulder and offer it to him. He grabs it away with a gracious nod and then sets his predator eyes back to the business of watching. I look at Mom and give her a raised eyebrow. She smiles and matches my eyebrow. We're both impressed.

And then Russ's back stiffens and he hisses, "Deer!"

Sure enough a doe has stepped onto the road that runs along the edge of the field. She is moving quickly, not running, but not a slow, normal walk either.

On the ride over, we agreed that Russ would take the first shot if he wanted. It turns out he's taken a shooting class and even won best shot at it.

My mom pushes off of her chair and eases to her knees next to him. She whispers questions and instructions to him. Russ nods or shakes his head, not daring to take his eyes off that doe. She is stepping quickly toward us.

With Mom's guidance, Russ raises his gun. I see the gun shaking. I remember those first deer nerves. Heck, I've killed four, and I still have those nerves.

The doe is still speed walking. I'd have already shot.

Russ whispers, "I need her to stop. I've only shot targets." His voice is quivery like his hands.

Mom whispers back, "Chloe will help. Just say when you're ready for the shot."

I unglove my hand and curl my pointer finger and thumb together, pressing them between my lips.

Russ nods. "Ready."

I blow out a sharp, shrill whistle. The doe stops in her tracks. She looks over right at our blind.

She's frozen in place, but I know she could blast off at any moment.

Ka-pow! Russ's body flinches with the recoil of his rifle. The doe collapses down onto her side. She doesn't move.

"Whoa, nice shot, Russ," I say. Shooting class or not, I'm surprised those shiver nerves didn't mess with his aim just a little.

Mom agrees and pats him on the back. Russ has an extra large smile radiating like the summer sun. I can't help but smile myself.

Russ's smile dims a little. "I'm going to need help gutting. I've never done that before."

"Don't worry, I'll help you," I say. It now feels like Russ is my younger brother or something — in a good way. I now know what Mom means when she says her favorite hunting trips have been with me, even though I've never gotten anything close to one of her trophy bucks.

"That's a good eating doe," I tell Russ. "My dad will want to make some of his *Famoriffic Venison Chilli* for dinner."

"*Famoriffic Chilli* tonight? From my deer?" I can't tell if he's excited or grossed out or something.

"Well, unless you don't like chilli," I say. "He can make other stuff, too."

"No, I love chilli. I just can't believe I hunted something we'll eat tonight. That's weird. And awesome."

"You think that's awesome? Just wait until you taste Dad's *Famoriffic Chilli*," I say.

"Yeah, I'm excited to try it," Russ says. Then his smile slips away, and he fixes me with a serious look. "Well, excited as long as the secret ingredient is not *buh-na-nuhs*." He sing-songs out a perfect impression of Dad.

Mom and I bust out laughing.

"No bananas," I tell Russ. And then I add that he can come hunting with us any time.

Opening
Morning Poem

Part 1

My grin is glued on.

Wisps of coffee sips linger on my breath.

The gray morning eases into daylight.

I'm engulfed by the sweet smell of

dead-leaf dirt.

I sneak glances at Dad,
sitting, wearing his grown up stone face.
So serious.
Waiting for a chance at the meat
that will fill our family's freezer.

Camo coveralls. Orange vest.
Matching hat.
His rifle rests across his tree-trunk legs.
My rifle rests across my twiggy branches.

Part 2

The cold slips icy fingers through my thermals,
gripping my flesh, my bones. I shiver.
My smile fades. My grin a grimace.
My legs numb.
I didn't know my butt could fall asleep,
but there it goes, nodding off.

I shift as quietly as possible.
I daydream of home. Other days
I'd still be a warm burrito in bed.
Should I tell Dad?

Will the great hunter be ready to go?
Can I face his face when I tell him that
I am so, so done?

His eyes are shut. Shut!
I envy his dream smile.
He's home here. Cozy in the cold.
I shift again quietly.
I'll let him sleep.
Ouchy pins and needles flash in waves
across my twiggy legs.
I beg them to wake up.
I thought hunting would be easier.

Part 3

The sun peeks out above the horizon.
The gray woods sparkle
with a frosted layer of icing.
A ray of heat blasts through the branches,
cooking my right side.
I'm tempted to roll my left into the rays,
like a marshmallow needing to brown
on the other side.

I stay still though.
This is hunting.

Part 4
I have heard nothing.
But I see wasps of breath clouds
back-lit by the sun.
Her steps still silent, the doe steps out.
My cold misery instantly forgotten.

I whisper. "Dad. Hey, Dad."
Heavy breaths. Quiet gravel snoring.
I'm the lone hunter. Alive with excitement.

I millimeter my gun into position.
I line up the sight like practice.
The sun in my veins,
I fire.

Dad wakes with a spasm.
The doe falls slowly to the ground.
The sweetness of dead-leaf dirt now spiced
with smokey gun powder.

Dad doesn't know.

I point.

His stone face eases into a smile.

Just like mine.

This year, I've filled our freezer.

Mom's Perfect Spot

I was in the woods a half hour before sunrise. Mom was letting me sit in her stand this year, and I wasn't going to waste the opportunity. This was the stand where she'd taken a trophy buck every year for six years straight. And it wasn't just luck or that she was patient, or that she was just an all around great hunter. She'd created, or "sculpted" as she said, the spot to funnel in mature bucks.

A field spread out to the right, planted half with soybeans and half with a food-plot blend of tasty deer treats. A hollow ran along to the left with a well-worn trail threading along the near ridge, lined with piles of comfort brush for the monsters to feel hidden as they traveled to and from their beds. And then, out in front, a mature growth of timber with underbrush cut back to create shooting lanes aiming out from the stand like spokes from the center of a wheel. I still couldn't believe she'd let me take her perfect spot while she'd be over in my stand behind the pond. She would be guaranteed a doe, but probably not another one of her trophies.

I hadn't been sitting long before I heard soft footsteps approaching. My pulse sped up a little. The dark woods still made me nervous even though I knew there was nothing to worry about. Last year, I'd about had a heart attack as

I'd heard loud leaf crackling steps coming right up to my treestand before my surroundings were lit enough to see anything. I had dug my pen light out and shined it down. A raccoon waddled along passing right beneath my stand on its way to splash around in the shallows of the pond. It had sounded big enough to be a bear.

This morning, the steps I now heard were not loud and crackling. They were more elusive. I heard a few steps in one place and then, a minute later, more of the same several yards away from where I'd heard them before. I suspected a deer.

There was dim morning light, but it just made the woods blend into a perfect dark, gray camouflage.

Two more steps. In front of me. Fifty or sixty yards out. I squinted. My eyes strained to take in enough light to see what was making the sounds.

A songbird suddenly burst into a morning melody in the tree next to me, and I about fell out of my treestand. Then another bird joined in and another as the woods began to wake up. The birds' chatter overwhelmed my hearing so that I couldn't make out any more steps. Even my eyes seemed less able to work as the songbirds overpowered my senses.

The light slowly brightened, and I could see two wide tree trunks flanked by a stand of cedars in the direction I had heard the steps. There was nothing else there. Perhaps the steps had been a squirrel scrounging for acorns.

I swept my gaze slowly to the right, taking in my view of the food plot and soybean field. It was brighter out there, so I could see a variety of birds flip-flapping around, some quarreling, some pecking the ground, some chirping away as if giving advice for the others to follow.

No deer though, so I slid my gaze back all the way across to my left, finding a still very dark hollow. A couple of squirrels were chattering as if upset about something. I smiled as I imagined them insulting all the singing birds around them for waking them up. It was too dark to see anything but the shadows of trees in that direction, so I kept straining to listen beyond the deafening songbirds, beyond the annoyed squirrels, beyond the woodpecker who suddenly echoed a vibrating beat from a tree off behind me.

And then a step. Or was it a step? The morning chatter still dominated, muting the crackle of leaves. I swept my gaze back in front. Wasn't that the right direction? I squinted my vision to the cedar grove. Nothing there. And then I refocused closer on the two large tree trunks, side by side. Something puzzled my brain. Something about that horizontal branch stretching behind but between them. Had that branch always been there?

Then it twitched an ear to the left of the two trunks. Just behind them. That wasn't a horizontal branch, but a deer's back cutting a line between the trees.

And antlers. My breath sucked in. A giant beam curved out above the twitched ear, and I now saw one eye. Watching me.

Was I holding my breath? I stayed still for longer than I thought possible. I couldn't raise my gun while being watched. I didn't have a shot anyway. The trees shielded him perfectly.

He stayed still for so long that I started to make his antler into a branch and the twitched ear into an unfallen leaf. He could be an illusion pieced together from the imagination of a too hopeful hunter.

Maybe if I eased my gun. Maybe I could get the scope on him. That would make him real. I'd have a chance if he ran.

I glanced down as I tightened my grip on my rifle and eased the stock to my shoulder. I looked back up. Gone.

The buck had melted into the brown-gray woods. He'd been there. The antler-branch was gone. The horizontal line had disappeared.

After lunch, Mom loaned me her grunt call. I didn't know if I'd use it since I never had before. She reviewed the different sounds I could make. When I tried, my deep grunt pitched over to a wounded goose honk. But she encouraged me to keep it anyway.

Sure enough, I practiced grunting just after I got back in the stand and did a perfect wounded goose honk. I'm sure it chased every deer out of the county. I swore off the thing and sat and watched as the afternoon inched by.

No deer came, but there was plenty to see. There was a chipmunk swimming in and out of a pile of leaves for a while. It was comical – like he was putting on a show for me. I struggled to watch the woods and not him. Later, a bluejay landed in a branch just feet from my own tree. He looked at me with bobbing, untrusting eyes before squawking as he flew away. After that a few crows flew from treetop to treetop, their suspicious caws reporting their findings to one another as they made their way overhead. It was actually really peaceful. Deer or not, I enjoyed the afternoon.

And then footsteps again. Heavy steps this time from behind me along the deep hollow. I figured it was raccoon. Or maybe a trespassing hunter tromping through the brush. No way a deer would make this much noise, that was for sure.

I turned and eased around the side of my tree and to my surprise here came a buck—perhaps the same buck—stomping along. My pulse pumped in my ears and nervous tingles spread across my chest. His nose was to the ground, his ears folded back, his neck swollen, and fur bristling. He was in full rut. Ready to find a doe. Ready to stomp on any other buck that got in his way.

I raised my rifle to my shoulder and slowly swung the barrel around to that side of the tree in anticipation of him continuing into range. I watched as he then dipped down into the brushy lip of that hollow off of the well-worn game trail. He picked a line that kept just his head and the very top of his back visible as he passed by me. I had his head in my scope. Nine tall and thick tines. Wide too. I thought about trying a head or neck shot, but I was counting on him breaking back up onto the game trail and into an opening. Any moment now.

The warmth in my chest turned to ice. I watched helplessly as he stepped across my last shooting lane still down in the hollow. I had no shot. And now, with an unbroken tangle of brushy brambles blocking me, he angled back up onto the trail as if he'd skirted me on purpose. Was he really that smart?

I heard him stomping off even after I lost sight of him. And then I remembered the grunt call. Mom had told me to give one semi-quiet, 6-second "hey, who goes there" grunt if I had a buck disappear on me again. This time I blew it out perfectly. No wounded goose.

The steps stopped. Or had he just continued out of earshot? I stared into the brambles he had crossed behind. My eyes darted all over that spot trying to pick out the movement of gray-brown fur. I was patient. I watched for 10 minutes. Or was it 20? No matter, because nothing whatsoever happened. He was gone.

I thought maybe another grunt call. One last pointless effort of bringing him back in. I ungloved my hands this time, thinking that handling the call perfectly would give me the best chance at a good sound. This was no time for a goose honk.

Ch-chuh crash! The sound of leaves exploding beneath stomping steps. I jerked my head to the right, catching a white flash of tail. A deer charging away from 20 yards. The buck.

I was stunned. He'd circled around down wind. He'd seen me take off my gloves. I wanted to toss those stupid gloves.

I gritted my teeth, but still marveled at the wide antlers disappearing across the field beyond the soybeans into the cluster of trees. My heart still beat fast as I sat there, both disappointed and thrilled.

Then, *ka-pow!* A rifle shot off in that direction. The pond stand. Mom! He'd run right to her. Now I was even more disappointed. And even more thrilled. Mom had gotten her trophy after all. I'd missed out again.

I waited for my cell phone to buzz. My cell phone always buzzed after Mom shot. She'd tell me she'd gotten a deer. A buck. My buck. I'd climb down and help her gut him like I always did. Maybe I'd joke that one of this buck's antlers belonged to me since my mistake had sent him running right to her. I smiled. Mom would think that was funny. And sad. How had I messed up this perfect spot?

Then right on cue my phone buzzed.

I answered with the hunting whisper she'd taught me. "Hey, Mom. You got him, huh?"

She whispered back. "No, a young doe. Still haven't seen any bucks. She'll be better eating anyway."

"You mean, you didn't see the..." That's the second I saw him.

"Gotta go," I whispered and hung up.

He was back. By those two trees again. In front this time. Broadside. His head was turned back and away. Watching the direction of Mom's shot.

I put the rifle to my shoulder. Thumbed the safety off. Instincts.

Ka-boom! I didn't remember seeing the crosshairs. Had I really squeezed the trigger?

The buck hop-jumped to the side. Stumbled. Then he charged off. He busted through the brambles and ran down into the hollow. Out of sight. Had I hit him? Had I missed?

Then I heard him crash. Down there in that hollow. He'd fallen. I'd gotten that trophy buck.

I smiled. A rush of relief spread all over me. It was my turn to call Mom.

Stupid
Squirrels

Grandpa once told me that while I sat out in the woods listening to the sound of crackling steps in the leaves that I needed to assume it was a deer even if I thought it was something else. Especially a squirrel.

At the time, I thought he was just messing with me. Little bouncy squirrels are not going to sound the same as a big, stompy deer.

But there I was, opening afternoon, sitting on the ground with my back pressed against a large oak. My pulse pumped with excitement for the thirtieth time because the step-crackle-crunch of a stupid squirrel sounded like it could be a deer approaching the mock scrape I'd freshly scented.

I was disciplined though. I'd hear the first distant steps on the dry leaves, then ease my gaze from the left to the right—no sudden movements—and glue my vision to the brush and trees that hid whatever animal was behind them.

The first ten times I just knew I'd soon see the brown fur—and perhaps even the white-tan tines—of a deer come strolling into sight.

Not so.

Instead, there would come a little puff of hyperactive rodent sifting through dead leaves for acorns and hickory nuts. I'd mentally mark it a squirrel in that location as the steps of a new mystery critter started off in the opposite direction. If I'd been squirrel hunting, the day would have been incredible. It seemed as though I'd sat down in the mother load of squirrel activity. But I was deer hunting, and it was frustrating as my marks on the mental map were getting jumbled, and I had to keep assuming there were deer approaching from all sides even though I knew they were just stupid squirrels.

Then, behind my tree, maybe five steps back, I suddenly heard a soft crunchy step. My breath sucked in. It sounded different this time. A deer. It had to be. I gripped the gun on my lap as I turned my neck and leaned to peek around the tree.

Another step in my direction. I was shaking a little. I just knew it was going to be a deer this time. Totally had to be a big, giant...

Squirrel! No way. The stupid thing had gotten me again. It was right there behind my tree with its face buried under a pile of leaves, and its poofy red tail waving away as if saying, "Haha, I'm not what you're waiting for, and I know it."

Then, a scritch-scritch-scratch from off to my left, and a second smaller squirrel was joining the first. The bigger guy chitter-chattered a complaint and lunged at the small guy. The small guy chitter-chattered and fled up onto a downed limb and jumped onto my tree in one big spasm. The big fellow chased, and I heard their scratchy steps climbing up the other side of my tree.

Which, to be honest, was kind of nerve-wracking and very cool at the same time. I didn't want them to fall down on top of me and scratch my face off or anything. But as long as they kept their squeaky game of chase up there in the branches it was entertaining to watch.

Especially when I heard another squirrel coming to join the fun. He step-crackle-crunched off to my left, and I eased my gaze over to see him bounce onto a smaller oak and dash up into the branches. Then this new squirrel ran and leaped from one of that tree's limbs onto a low branch just over my head. I gave a mental hip-hip-hooray for his pretty amazing circus act. Then he flashed onto the trunk and up and across to join in the round and round game of tag the first two were still playing.

I don't know what kind of switch the first two had flipped, but more squirrels were headed in for the fun. Two more came step-crackle-crunching in, chasing each other up the back side of my tree. I swirled myself around and I could crane my neck back to watch the little dudes going crazy right there above my head. It was down right fun to watch.

Fun right up until the goofballs came dashing down my side of the trunk and headed right toward my face. I flinched and sort of instinctively gave a "chuch-chuch" call at them as if I knew how to say "Stop right there!" in Squirrel.

But it worked because the one in the lead suddenly stopped as the others all sort of froze in a line behind him. The lead squirrel was only two feet above me. Two feet from dropping down to claw out my eyes. The others, on that low limb right behind, seemed ready to cheer him on.

I was frozen in place trying to decide whether shoeing my hand up at him would scare him off or signal his face-eating attack. And if that wasn't enough, I heard another squirrel coming in from behind me. Well, behind me because I was all turned around looking up into the tree, but this one was actually step-crackle-crunching in from the front of my spot. If he was going to join his buddies for the chasing party, he'd have to bounce right into my lap to get there. I was surrounded.

Oh great, I thought. Death by squirrel. My heart was pumping. My hands began to shake. I could hear the new squirrel step-crackle-crunching up to my mock scrape. The squirrel in the tree shifted his stare away from me to the approaching one. Then he and the others in the tree blasted into a chorus of chatters as they turned and fled upward. They all dashed out onto separate branches and squeaked down at the new squirrel behind me as if they were mad that he'd decided to crash their party.

Or as if he wasn't welcome, which is when it hit me.

This wasn't another squirrel.

I stayed frozen, looking up, flipping through the list of possible animals it could be. I super-slow-motioned my head back around. There in front of me was a beautiful buck. He flinched and shifted his eyes directly upon me.

My shoulders deflated like punctured balloons. I'd been watching the stupid squirrels while this amazing buck had walked up to my mock scrape exactly as I'd planned and hoped and dreamed.

The buck stared at me. He stayed as still as a stone. He knew something was off, but my presence hadn't clicked for him yet.

He snorted and stomped a hoof.

I mentally cursed at myself. It was over. He was a moment away from puzzling out my form. There was no way I could pull up my gun without spooking him. Still, I had to try. I gripped my rifle.

That's all it took.

The buck bolted, exploding like a race horse, busting through the brush, so that even though I threw my gun up, I couldn't land him in my scope for even a second.

And just like that, he was gone, leaving me behind, sitting beneath the mocking chatter of those stupid, stupid squirrels.

The Deerbler

I sat at the cabin table listening to Uncle Tim's story. I sure was enjoying hearing about somebody else seeing a deer. My first day ever at deer camp, and Dad and I had seen jack squat.

He said, "I'm patting my coat pockets. My pants. Nothing. I must have forgot my durn shells back here in the cabin. Gotta be the biggest buck in Twain County just keeps a coming in, and I ain't got noth'n but an empty rifle to point at 'em. He walks right in and then plops down under my stand for a nap."

"Whoa," I said.

"I know. That's what I was thinking. 'Whoa. Maybe I should try to jump down there and put the ole sleeper hold on.' I know it was a stupid idea, but I was frustrated. So, I'm all quiet, bending forward to see under my treestand, and you know the shells that I thought I'd left in the cabin?"

"Yeah," I answer, my mouth wide with awe.

"I guess I hadn't checked all my pockets, because three of 'em fall out of my chest pocket and drop right onto his head. He must of thought the sky was falling cause he jumped up and tore off like the Little Red Hen."

Dad cut in. "You mean Henny Penny." He was shaking his head chuckling to himself as he stirred the pot of beans on the stove.

"Henny what?" Uncle Tim asked.

Dad sighed. "Henny Penny thought the sky was falling. You said the Little Red Hen. She couldn't get any help with the chores. And man do I know how she felt." He shot us a serious look followed by a smile as he grabbed an oven mitt and checked the rolls.

Uncle Tim acted like somebody had just slapped him across the face. "Brother, you know better than to interrupt a man at the apex of a hunt'n story." He said it all offended, but he and Dad always played around like that.

"You're right, I'm so sorry," Dad said, mockingly. "Climax, not apex, by the way."

Uncle Tim picked an orange up off the table and threw it at Dad's back. "That'll teach you. Next time I'll find a watermelon to throw." He turned back to me. "Anyway, where was I?"

"The buck took off," I said.

"Oh yeah. So, he's running away and I'm grabbing for a shell in case I can get it loaded and a shot off in time. But that's not gonna happen. My chest pocket is empty because I just dropped the only three shells I had on the buck's head."

"Wow," I say. "That's crazy."

"You're telling me. Try being the fella who watches the biggest buck he's ever seen disappear out of sight. Actually, I'm surprised you didn't see him. He ran off in your direction."

"No we didn't see a thing," I said. I looked at him amazed. I couldn't believe that big buck was in the same woods as me that morning.

Dad sighed. "You sure see a lot of biggest bucks."

Uncle Tim shook his head. "Don't listen to your Dad. He's just jealous of my hunt'n skills. I attract them big bucks like flies on..."

The cabin door suddenly flew open, and my big brother stormed in. He stumbled over to the table out of breath.

"You aren't gonna believe it." He sat down, his eyes still wide like he'd seen a ghost.

Uncle Tim scooted his chair closer to the table. "What happened, Scotty? Did you see the big one? I didn't hear any shots."

"Oh, I saw the big one all right," he said. He looked at me. A wild look of excitement. He whispered, "I saw the Deerbler."

"You saw the Deerbler," Uncle Tim slapped Scotty on the back. "Tell us about it, Boy. Tell us what you saw."

Dad turned back to the stove shaking his head.

"What's a deerbler?" I asked.

"Not a deerbler," answered Uncle Tim. "The Deerbler. There's only one. I heard about him from some fellers and told Scotty about it last year."

"Yeah." Scotty nodded. "And he was just like Uncle Tim described. Part buck deer. Part gobbler turkey. The ultimate hunter's dream."

"What?" I said. "I've never heard of that." I said it skeptically, but I was already picturing it in my head.

"I looked it up on the internet and some folks think a scientist was doing some genetic experiments, and the Deerbler got out," Scotty said.

Uncle Tim cut in. "No, I heard it was a bolt of lightening. Fused the two together."

Scotty raised his hands over his head. "But I never believed it was really real let alone that I'd see him."

I had tingles all over. Scotty was so excited. I'd never seen him so excited.

"The sun was behind the trees. I was starting to consider leaving when he just appeared out in the field. At first I just saw his antlers. Huge antlers. Probably a 20 pointer or so. Typical. That got my heart pumping right there."

"Well, yeah," said Uncle Tim. "I've only seen one 20 pointer in all of my years, and I almost had a heart attack."

My heart was pounding just listening. My day had been so boring. I couldn't believe all of this had been going on, and I hadn't seen a thing.

"I put my scope on him and that's when I saw the beard. Thirty inch beard puffing out of his neck. And wings."

"Wings?!" Uncle Tim threw his hat down on the table. "I was hoping he had wings."

"Oh, he had wings alright. And a tail. No white tail. A long turkey tail. Fanned it out right then and there and started strutting and drumming."

I could feel my eyes about to pop as I imagined the Deerbler strutting out there in front of Scotty. Gosh, I was so jealous.

"Why didn't you shoot it?" I asked. "I mean, you didn't get him right?"

"That's a good question. You see, I was about to. I had a perfect shot on him as he strutted out there. But I got myself to wondering about the season. Was he legal in deer season or turkey season? I'm no poacher you know."

"Oh, man." Uncle Tim laughed. "I never thought about that."

"Yeah." Scotty nodded, that serious excitement still plastered on his face. "Then he grobbled."

"Grobbled?" I whispered.

"Yeah, grobbled. Not quite a grunt. Not quite a gobble. A grobble. And then he stretched his wings and flew up to roost. You should have seen him perched up there on that big branch."

"Tarnation! I know nobody ever heard him grobble or seen him roost before." Uncle Tim was laughing and pounding a fist on the table. "Scotty, this has got to be the greatest hunt'n story I ever heard."

"Yeah, the greatest story ever," Dad said, still turned around at the stove stirring the beans.

"No, not a story," Scotty said. He got out his cell phone and pulled up a photo. "I took pictures."

"Pictures?" Uncle Tim stopped laughing.

Dad dropped the spoon into the pot. "I've got to see this."

We all gathered around. Sure enough, there was the silhouette of a giant buck with a turkey beard, wings and fanned-out tail, strutting out in the middle of the field. And then another one of him roosting up in a big oak tree. No doubt about it, the Deerbler was real.

Uncle Tim was totally confused. "What the?"

Dad just stood there with his eyes squinted, staring like he does when he's working on a crossword puzzle.

The thing was the most awesome animal I'd ever seen. Definitely any hunter's dream. Until I noticed the sky.

"Wait a second. There weren't any clouds today. You faker!" His pictures had big puffy clouds in the background. He must have taken them last season or something. "You doctored those." Scotty was good with doing stuff like that on the computer.

"What do you mean? That's the real deal." He was smiling now. Everyone was smiling.

"Good stuff, Son." Dad went back to the beans. "I admit, you had me for a second there."

Uncle Tim was shaking his head now. "Holy cow, I'm gonna have to throw in the towel on my stories. I can't compete with technology."

Scotty started laughing now. He looked at me. "You have to admit I had you going, too."

"Whatever," I crossed my arms over my chest. He sure did have me going, but I didn't need him to know that. "I'm the one who figured it out."

"You're so gullible though. If it had only been cloudy today. Dang weather."

"I am not gullible."

He beamed. It didn't matter what I said now. I just promised myself he wouldn't ever get me like that again and changed the subject.

"Hey, Dad. How much longer on the beans?"

"Almost done, hold your horses."

"I'm not rushing you. I was just wondering if I had time to go practice my snipe calls. Uncle Tim, you're still taking me after supper, right?"

"Oh yeah," Uncle Tim answered. "Now the thing about snipe calling is..."

Safety First

A monster buck walks into the field 300 yards away. I glass him through my binoculars and count 8—wait no—10 thick tall tines. My heart kicks against my ribs, and I hold back an overwhelming desire to "Yahoo!" He's so far out of range for me, but I've never seen a buck anywhere near his size. Unless I count on TV or hanging on the wall at the outdoor gear shop, which is where this guy belongs. He's so impressive.

My stand sits back 15 or so yards into a cluster of trees along a drainage creek. Several does have been grazing out in the field for an hour. They're 100 yards out. I could make that shot with the 30-06 I hold in my lap, but I've been waiting for a buck. Waiting for the dude I'm now watching strut out away from the trees. He's headed for those does.

I gulp and feel my goofy smile widen as my body begins to tremble a little. I can't believe he's coming in. I'm going to be like a total hunting legend at school.

My brother said he'd give me 50 dollars if I downed a buck bigger than his. Lucky for him I didn't take the bet. Up until a minute ago, it would have totally been a dream to down an 8 pointer. Now his buck seems small.

The big buck just keeps walking. Angling toward those does without any hesitation. I expect him to stop and sniff the air. Catch my scent, maybe. Turn and run. That's what happens to me every season. Something messes up. But not this time.

He's 200 yards away now. Through the binoculars he looks angry – like a bull at a rodeo. Nothing is going to stop this guy. He's mine. He's going to be mine.

Something suddenly flashes into my view through the binoculars. I pull them away and see the group of does running and flagging. At first, my heart sinks. I'm busted. But they're running right toward me. Or toward the heavily used trail along the drainage creek that passes me at 30 yards. They're fleeing from the buck. They're playing hard to get, yet luring him right to me. It's getting even better.

I look back to the buck. He's still coming. Angling directly my way now. I still wait even though he's within my range. I go ahead and raise my rifle and find him in the scope. If he starts to run, I'll still have a shot. Otherwise, I'll let him come in for a sure shot. He's at 100 yards now. I'm good at that distance. But even better at 50. I might as well let him come right to me.

I hear the does come crashing into the leaves and prance down the trail beside me. I don't even glance at them. I watch the buck keep coming.

And he does. He's close enough that the fur on his chest fills the scope. I center the crosshairs below his neck, imagining his heart right there. I'm steadier than I thought I'd be. Easy breaths. The moment has come.

I squeeze the trigger.

Nothing. Nothing happens.

I watch the crosshairs quake around and then settle them again over his heart. He's still walking my way. I set the crosshairs. Pull the trigger.

Nothing. Again.

Questions flash around as I truly begin to shake now. I pull the rifle down and look at the bolt. It is set. I know it's loaded. Did I bump the gun as I climbed into my stand? Did my brother sabotage it while I slept last night? It has to work. I need to make it work.

I slap the bolt to make sure it had locked down all the way. Once while target practicing it wouldn't fire because I'd failed to engage it all the way down.

I raise the rifle again. Oh no! The buck has stopped. I'm hidden. Well hidden. But still, has he seen me?

No, not me. Another buck has left the woods off to my right. My eyes could explode out of my head. He's huge too. 10 points. Maybe bigger than the first one. Yeah, bigger than the first.

I shoulder the gun and find the new buck in the scope. My whole body shivers, and I pull at my rifle with all of my strength to settle my shakes. I get steady. Find his heart. Tug the trigger.

Nothing. Tug again. Nothing. Yank, yank on the trigger. It won't shoot! I want to throw the thing. I want to throw up.

Instead I relax the rifle to my lap, needing to settle myself down. I watch the bucks size each other up. Lower their heads, and Crash! The bucks lock antlers and drive against one another.

Clack-crash. Clack-crack crash. They grunt and strain and shove back and forth, twisting their powerful necks at each other, locked in a violent sumo match. I'm absolutely in awe, having a front row seat to such an amazing sight. I'm half relieved I hadn't been able to shoot.

Then I hear a herd of crashing steps coming in from behind. I look and see the does prancing back this way. They cut across the creek and under my stand. Stopping, they look back the way they'd come. I look, too, and almost faint.

The grandaddy of all bucks is walking down the game trail. Swaying like the stud he knows he is. A giant nest of points and knobs shoot off his hulking beams.

The does crash off in the other direction, but he ignores them. His attention is on the two fighting bucks as he walks the trail past me at 30 yards. I ease the gun up again, expecting it to magically work this time. I pull the trigger.

Nothing! Nothing! Nothing!

I want to slam it against the tree. I want to slam myself against the tree. And yet, through all the frustration, I'm also thrilled to be there.

The granddaddy buck stops at the edge of the cluster of trees. The other bucks are still 50 yards out, still crunching their antlers together.

I take a deep, deep breath and stare down at my gun. Okay, I sighted the thing in last weekend. I hadn't had to make any adjustments because it was perfect. Then I cleaned it. Even now I had to admire how shiny new the whole thing was even though it was Grandpa's old rifle. Even his little yellow "Be safe" sticker is shiny there below the open sight.

The safety! I almost slap myself in the forehead. Duh. I've been forgetting to take the safety off.

The granddaddy deer still stands at the edge of the trees facing away. I raise my gun again and pull it extra tight against my shoulder to settle a fresh set of nervous shakes. He's mine.

I raise my thumb and push the safety off. *Click*.

Grandaddy throws his head around and looks right up at me. Then he turns and sprints out and away along the edge of the field. I try to lock him in my sight, but he's too fast, and there's too much brush. He disappears. No shot! I can't believe he'd heard the click, but no time to think about that.

I sling the barrel of my rifle back over to the fighting bucks. They aren't there. Wait, there they go. Two white tails bounce away side by side. Spooked. Out of range. And gone.

I sit there trembling. How could I have messed up with the three biggest bucks ever in front of me at the same time?

It is a good thing I didn't actually bet my brother 50 dollars. That would be about one dollar for every antler point I just watched run away. He'll laugh at me when I tell him what happened. Maybe I'll keep it to myself. No, there's no way I can keep this story to myself.

I shake my head and click the safety back on, knowing I will never—and I mean NEVER—forget to click it off again.

Zombie Deer

I've watched hunting shows for as long as I can remember and want so badly to be one of those famous hunters. Which was what I was thinking about as the 8 pointer took two more steps, and his head went behind a tree. This was my moment.

I held my bow steady, drawing back and leaning at the waist. It felt a little awkward balancing like that in my treestand, but I stood stable and ready. The buck continued out on the other side of the tree and stopped just enough beyond the tree for a nice shot at about 20 yards.

I knew Dad would be surprised as he watched through his video camera. I'd talked him into filming me from a separate treestand just behind me to the left. He thought my desire to be a famous deer hunter was on the ridiculous side and filming me was a waste of time at this point since I'd never killed a buck. That was about to change.

I squinted into my peep site, setting the glowing green peg over the kill zone. I hoped Dad was getting all of it. I hoped the video would look as perfect as it felt being there. We'd load it on Hunter WebTV, and I'd be on my way to famous.

I breathed slowly and eased the trigger of my release.

Swish! The arrow shot away.

Twing! A slight glance off a narrow branch. I'd looked right past the stupid thing.

The arrow ricocheted high and left, though, and *Thonk!* A hit. I'd nailed the buck right in the head. He swayed to one side. Then the other. And buckled at the knees, crashing to the ground. Lifeless.

"Whoa," I said aloud and then remembered the camera filming me. I didn't know what to say. I was excited, but it was a total screw up. Nobody shoots an arrow at a deer's head.

I swiveled around and shrugged my shoulders. "That's one way to kill a deer." And then grinned. I'd read an article online about talking to the camera as if I was prepared for anything that happened. It'd help the audience think of me as an expert. I thought I'd covered my ricochet shot pretty well.

Dad said, "Cut." Then set the camera down with a shake of his head. "Son, I told you to trim all those branches off of that tree."

"I got him, Dad. That's what counts."

"What counts to you is trying to be famous. You need to worry more about a sure and safe kill." He sounded annoyed, but not angry.

"That could have just as easily wounded him. You got lucky."

I sighed and imitated his deep voice. "Geez, Son, what a horrible thing you did dropping your first buck. I'm so disappointed in you."

He frowned. "I'm just saying that if you want to take the hunting show thing seriously, you better work more on the skills that make a good hunter and worry less about becoming an instant celebrity."

"So I looked through a twig. It happens. And the glancing head shot could be that unique thing to make it go viral on the web. This hunt rocked, I don't care what you say."

I smiled, already lost in a daydream about my future as a famous hunter. I gathered my gear to climb down. Dad collected his gear as he shook his head some more.

Once on the ground, Dad set up his tripod while I positioned the buck. There were just a few drops of blood on the fur where the arrow had crowned him in the brain and bounced off.

As I knelt there, Dad's advice sunk in. He was right. Sending a wounded deer off to suffer because I'd been too lazy to trim my shooting lane would make me feel sick inside. I promised myself that I'd never do it again. I nodded and grinned, realizing what a powerful moment it was. I'd have to reenact my thoughts for the camera. You know, reflecting on the hunt, learning from my mistakes. That's what the famous guys did and here I'd done it naturally off camera. Just another example of why I needed my own show; I was a natural.

When Dad was ready, I set my bow in the antlers and straddled the buck's back, kind of like riding a horse. I grabbed the antlers and pulled his head to a raised position.

"There, how does that look?" I asked.

"Seriously?" he asked. "You want to do this on top of him? That's kind of... I don't know..."

"...Awesome," I said, cutting him off. "Just hit record." Geez, he had no sense of showmanship.

Dad just shook his head again as he bent over the camera. "Action."

I smiled and got ready to speak when suddenly the dead buck shook his head back and forth a few times like clearing away cobwebs. Then he vibrated a set of groggy groan-grunts that rumbled around his whole body beneath me.

Fear exploded all over my body as I sat there frozen. In shock. I still gripped his main beams and flashed through mental questions about how a dead deer could shake his head and make creepy rumble sounds. And then it clicked.

"Zombie deer!" I shouted to Dad, who was bent over the camera.

He looked up from the viewfinder and threw his hands in the air. "Stop screwing around. I'm so close to done right now." And then he bent back down.

What game did he think I was playing? Deer puppet-head?

"Recording still," he said, impatiently.

An earthquake erupted beneath me as the buck launched straight up into a standing position. No doubt about it. He was 100%

undead zombie deer. Which was the moment I realized that I didn't believe in zombie deer and that the buck was truly undead in the "still alive" sort of way. My arrow had just knocked him out.

My heart was pumping fear all over my body, but one clear thought flashed to the forefront of everything else, This is the moment. I'm going to be famous. I grasped those main beams tighter, sitting upright and squeezing my legs into the buck's ribs as if riding a horse bareback. I'd make this moment last as long as I could.

The buck stood there for a moment, huffing in and out these angry sounding snort wheezes. I kept thinking how awesome it must look on camera. I checked for the flashing red light that signaled it was still recording.

Then, I looked over at Dad, who was standing with his jaw dropped open and his hands grasping the hat on his head. He looked so panicked that my electric fear flashed over me again. I thought if he was that scared, maybe I should go ahead and jump off. He stepped toward me and shouted, "Let go! Jump!"

That unfroze the buck. He whirled around. I slid backward and pancaked against his spine, my face buried against his shoulders. I clenched my hands tighter around the base of his antlers.

I heard Dad shout again, "Let go!" as the deer tore off with such incredible speed and strength that all I could do was slam up and down against his bony back like a human cape.

The fun was over; I wanted to let go now. I just didn't know how. I mean, I was afraid to just release my hands and fall off his hind-end because I knew I'd be hoof-kicked in the spleen or something on the way to the ground. As I tried to push off with my feet I just kept slipping and slamming into his back again.

All I could do was hang on for dear life —no pun intended. The underbrush and low branches grabbed at me as if echoing dad's calls to "Just let go!" And yet somehow in the jumbled chaos, I knew every second made the video that much better.

I bounced along for about thirty yards, my grip was starting to weaken, and we suddenly came to the fence. The buck rocketed straight up in the air like they do. My face crashed into his neck and I tasted a mouthful of grungy fur.

Then he angled straight back down. As his front legs landed, my body stayed up, and I flip-twisted over into a handstand. I floated, suspended in air above the buck for a slow-motion moment as if performing some bicycle stunt over the handlebars.

His head dropped down, my hands ripped away from his antlers, and my momentum rotated me forward.

"Ahhhhh!" I screamed like a crazed wildcat, expecting antlers to come stabbing up through my spine in the next moment.

I continued flipping, revolving around and mysteriously—amazingly—dropped onto my feet on the other side of the fence. I bounced a few steps, catching myself, but somehow landed standing.

My chest heaved with relieved breaths as I watched the buck streak away across the field. And I didn't care that my bow was still hanging there clanging around in his antlers.

Dad came running up from behind. "Oh, my gosh, are you okay?"

I shrugged. I couldn't speak. I felt like I'd been punched by a thousand fists. I shook so badly I thought I might collapse. I crumpled down into a sitting position.

Dad scrambled over the fence. "Son! Son, are you okay?"

I took two more deep breaths and then answered. "Yeah, I'm okay."

"Oh thank goodness," he hugged me tightly, and I realized he had tears on his cheeks. "I can't believe you're not hurt. Heck, I can't believe you're alive."

I said, "Dad, I'm okay, really." And then I half-smiled, remembering the camera. "And oh my gosh, do you know how awesome that video is going to be?"

Dad stared at me like I'd literally lost my head. Then he turned and clambered back over the fence, mumbling something about my being a famous rodeo clown.

But I wasn't listening. I was too busy thinking about all of the companies that would be calling and fighting to sponsor my hunting show.

I Am the Woods

I step to the edge of the morning woods.

To wait.

To settle.

My nose itches.

The potent perfume of damp fallen leaves.

Their unfallen brothers and sisters flutter

in the beautiful blinding mist.
I move forward.
The breeze on my face.
Always at my face.
The string dangling from my bow
whispers the wind's direction
even when it is difficult to feel.
I deer-step.
Crich-crunch. Crich-crunch.
Toe-heel. Toe-heel.
My heartbeat slows to the rhythm of the wild.
I tune my antennae of senses.
Mute the flirtatious songs of birds overhead.
Ignore shouts of squirrels calling me
an intruder.
I am the woods.

I scan the undergrowth
for flicks of movement.
Double check clusters of chaotic angles
for spots of brown or white fur.
Inspect a horizontal line with my binoculars.
Nothing.

I stalk to the top of the ridge
and press my back against a tree.
My camouflage fuses.
I am the woods.

My father shared this spot with me.
Where I can see far through the timber
across the wide hollow below.
Where the deer bed down often.
His father had known this, too.
I imagine centuries.
Other boys. Other men.
Standing where I stand.
Hunting where I hunt.
I am the woods.

I check the wind-string before moving.
The light breeze remains in my face.
I'll descend into the hollow.
But first, my binoculars.
One last look around.
I suddenly see him.
A spot I'd examined several times before.

Now the puzzle pieces fit.
There. His ears.
There. His head.
There. His tines.
Sitting motionless
within barriers of underbrush.
He is the woods.

No way of stalking in close enough.
No way an arrow gets through.
The lip of the ridge hides my withdrawal.
A predator with a plan.
Sixty yards in reverse. Then a circle.
The same hollow, but different.
Here it is narrow.
A natural funnel for his approach.
I find my place.
Kneel between a downed tree
and a standing oak.
I am the woods.

My heart quickens.
A deep breath as I raise my sheds.

Two mismatched antlers
dropped by separate bucks.
Slam.
Together.
Twist and pull.
Slam. Twist. Twist. Pull.
Two fighting bucks.
Heads coming together.
Slam. Twist. Twist. Pull.
Such a long minute.
I put down the antlers.
Pick up my bow.
Arrow nocked.
Deep breath.
Rapid heartbeat.
Impossible to calm.
A songbird flutters by.
A woodpecker rattles.
The sound of nothing.
And then something.
Steps.
Maybe.
Yes. Quick steps.

Beyond the narrow pass.
I raise my bow.
I am the woods.

Antlers emerge.
Eight. Counted without thinking.
Deep breath. Seeking the impossible calm.
He walks into full view.
Searches for those fighting bucks.
Stomps leaves. Steps closer.
Stops.
Looks my way.
Right at me.
Right through me.
I am the woods.

I trigger the release.
The blur of orange fletchings flash away.
Thunk. Into him.
He stumbles. Catches himself. Spins.
Rushes back beyond the pass.
Running steps. Fading steps.
Crash.

A moment of thrashing.
Then nothing.
The thunder of my heartbeat.
Then the birds.
The woodpecker.
The squirrels.
The leaf perfume upon the breeze.
I wait here a while.
Inside the wild beauty.
I am the woods.

About the Author

Michael Waguespack is the co-author and illustrator of the picture books *My First Deer Hunt*, *My First Turkey Hunt*, and *My First Fishing Trip*. He is a former elementary and middle school teacher with a Master of Fine Arts in Creative Writing for Children. He is an experienced hunter but admits that his fictional characters are often more successful than he is. He lives in Missouri with his wife and children.

Author Visits

Michael enjoys visiting schools. Tell your teacher and librarian to check out author visit information at

www.countrykidpublishing.blogspot.com

Made in the USA
Middletown, DE
10 December 2021